$\mathcal{N}$ ip! Nip! Mother Bear awoke

to two sharp nips on her big furry ears. Every

morning, growling fiercely, her two cubs tugged and

pulled at her to wake her. She sighed then huffed,

playfully giving in.

And her cubs squealed with joy and excitement.

"Will we finally go outside the den today?"

"Yes," she said as she led them out of the den for

the very first time.

"This new world looks so BIG!" the smaller cub said, a tiny bit scared as he peeked outside.

"Yes it is," Mother Bear agreed, gently pushing the cubs forward with her nose. The cubs blinked in the bright daylight, trying to see all the new colors and hear all the new sounds.

$\mathcal{T}$he cubs were a little clumsy but they padded forward on their soft paws.

They sniffed everything! The rocks and the trees and the grass and the flowers.

There were a thousand new smells for their noses.

Suddenly, Mother Bear stood on her hind legs, staring into the nearby underbrush. She sniffed the wind and then snorted very loudly! Without even thinking, the cubs scampered up a tall tree and looked down at her from the safety of a crooked limb.

Mother Bear stayed still for a moment and the cubs were completely silent.

$\mathcal{T}$hen Mother Bear relaxed and looked up at her cubs. "Good job, my little ones. Although there is no danger this time, you will always need to react quickly to my warnings."

*E*verything beneath them seemed small and far away. A bird landed near them and then, startled to see bears in a tree, flew away.

Mother Bear said, "And now you see that, while we cannot fly, bears can reach high and safe places. When you are far from the den and need a place to hide, you will always have the trees.

"That is what bears do."

"We are climbers."

*O*nce they were back on the ground,

the smaller cub followed a caterpillar. Then

the larger cub found a soft mushroom.

"May we eat it, Mother?" the cubs begged.

"Trust in your senses. What do your noses say?" Mother Bear asked.

"It smells bad. Our noses say to stay away!" the cubs squealed loudly.

Mother Bear nodded and said, "If you had eaten it, that mushroom would have made you very sick. Always trust your nose. Now, let's see if you can find us something good to eat."

$\mathcal{A}$ll of a sudden, their noses were filled with a delicious smell. And they heard buzzing above them. They had found a beehive!

$\mathcal{M}$other Bear was proud of them and said, "The bees give us honey, and it will become one of your favorite things to eat."

"You will always be able to find food

in the forest, just by following your nose,

Mother Bear continued.

"That is what bears do."

"We are searchers."

"May we try some honey?" the little cubs begged.

"You must be very careful, because bees can hurt even big bears like us," Mother warned.

But the two cubs were already clambering up the tree to stick their paws into the hive. The smaller bear poked his nose into the tree hole and came out with a face full of honey.

"M-M-M! It's different than Mother's milk. We like it," said the cubs.

The nearby buzzing was getting louder and louder. Suddenly, the larger cub howled, "OWWWW!" He covered his tender ears and quickly scrambled down the tree.

"Follow me!" Mother Bear growled and began to run through the forest. The cubs ran at her heels as fast as they could, all the way to the lake.

19

$\mathcal{M}$other Bear plunged into

the cool water and began paddling

toward the far side.

The little cubs hesitated at the edge. But even

louder buzzing and another "OWWWW!" made

them jump in to get away from the bees.

"Oh Mother, where are we?" they wondered.

"This is a lake. It provides us with many foods

and lots of fun. And now that you have crossed

it, we know that you can swim.

"That is what bears do."

"We are swimmers."

$\mathcal{B}$y the time they reached the other side of the lake, the bees had given up and were gone.

Mother Bear shook herself while her cubs played in the water.

"We are still so very hungry," the little cub called out to her.

23

"Well then, we will just have to find something to eat that can't hurt us!" Mother Bear said.

The cubs followed her along the shore. And they watched carefully. She uprooted cattails and other reeds and showed the cubs the juicy roots. They nibbled at them, but the strange new food was not as good as the milk they were used to.

"Soon you will love these new foods! Every bear is born with four big paws and you will learn to dig up the best part of roots and reeds to fill your hungry bellies.

"That is what bears do."

"We are diggers."

$\mathcal{T}$hen Mother Bear led her family back to
the cozy den. The cubs were very glad to see it
once again. She nuzzled and warmed her cubs
snug against her.

"I am so proud of you. You were very good
bears and you have learned so much today."

"But there is much more to learn, and tomorrow we will begin again," she said softly as she lovingly licked each cub.

"Because that is what Mother Bears do."

"We are teachers."

Mother Bear nursed her cubs until they were full and happy. "Such a big day for such big cubs," Mother Bear said. "The best thing you can do now to grow even bigger and stronger is to sleep.

"That is what bears do."

"We are sleepers."

We are climbers.

We are searchers.

We are swimmers.

We are diggers.

We are teachers.

We are sleepers.

"We are bears."

Cover design by Russell S. Kuepper

NorthWord Books for Young Readers
11571 K-Tel Drive
Minnetonka, MN 55343
1-888-255-9989
www.tnkidsbooks.com

Library of Congress Cataloging-in-Publication Data
Grooms, Molly.
   We are bears / text by Molly Grooms ; illustrations by Lucia Guarnotta.
      p. cm.
   Summary: When Mother Bear and her two cubs leave the den for the first time they practice behaviors including climbing, searching, swimming, digging, and finally sleeping.
   ISBN 1-55971-836-6 (softcover)
   1. Bears--Juvenile fiction.   [1. Bears--Fiction. 2. Animals--Infancy--Fiction.]   I. Guarnotta, Lucia, ill. II. Title.
   PZ10.3.J93 We 2000
   [E]--dc21
                              00-028350

Printed in Singapore
10 9 8 7 6 5